Alice in Wonderland

A SIENA BOOK

Siena is an imprint of Parragon Books

Published by Parragon Book Service Ltd.
Units 13-17, Avonbridge Trading Estate,
Atlantic Road, Avonmouth, Bristol BS11 9QD

Produced by The Templar Company plc, Pippbrook Mill,
London Road, Dorking, Surrey RH4 1JE

Copyright © 1996 Parragon Book Service Limited

Designed by Mark Kingsley-Monks

All rights reserved.

Printed and bound in Italy

ISBN 0-75251-276-5

Alice in Wonderland

Illustrated by Carole Gray
Retold by Dugald Steer

SIENA

Alice was sitting by the riverbank, feeling very bored. Suddenly she saw a White Rabbit run past.

"I shall be late, I shall be late!" he said, looking at his watch.

Alice followed him, and fell down a very deep hole, full of shelves and cupboards.

At the bottom of the hole Alice found a bottle. She drank from it and became very small. Then she ate a little cake and grew very big! She cried so much that when she grew small again she nearly drowned in her own tears.

There were some animals swimming in Alice's tears. They all swam to the bank and had a race to dry off.

After the race Alice found the White Rabbit's house. But he wasn't at home.

"How will I ever get to be the right size?" Alice wondered.

Outside she found a sleepy caterpillar smoking a strange pipe on a mushroom.

"This mushroom will make you the right size!" he said.

And it did.

Nearby there was a house. Inside Alice found a Duchess looking after a baby, a Cheshire Cat with a big grin, and an angry Cook who was throwing things around the kitchen.

"Here," said the Duchess. "You can nurse the baby. I must go and play croquet with the Queen."

Alice carried the baby outside. She was very surprised when it turned into a little pig.

"It was an ugly baby," said Alice, "but it's a beautiful pig!"

Alice saw the Cheshire Cat, grinning at her from a tree.

The Cat gradually started to disappear, starting at its tail. Its grin was the last thing to go.

"How very odd!" said Alice.

Soon Alice arrived at a tea party. She sat down to tea with a Mad Hatter, a Mad March Hare and a little Dormouse who was asleep.

"There's no room!" they cried.

"There's plenty of room!" said Alice, but they were so rude that she left anyway. As she went, the Hatter and the Hare tried to stuff the Dormouse into a teapot!

Next, Alice came to a garden. The gardeners were painting a white rose with red paint.

"We made a mistake!" they said. "If the Queen finds out she will be very angry!"

At that moment the Queen of Hearts arrived.

"Off with their heads!" she shouted to her soldiers.

"Get to your places!" shouted the Queen. It was time for the croquet game.

Alice was surprised to see that the balls were really hedgehogs, the mallets were flamingos and the arches were soldiers! Stranger still, the soldiers looked as if they were made from playing cards.

Soon the Queen was shouting "Off with his head!" to everyone.

After the game Alice went to the beach where she met a Gryphon and a sad Mock Turtle. He was sad because he wasn't a real Turtle. Together, they danced a rather funny dance for Alice called the Lobster Quadrille, and sang her a rather strange song.

The Gryphon took Alice to the Court of Justice. The Knave of Hearts was on trial for stealing some jam tarts.

"Off with her head!" cried the Queen, looking at Alice.

"What rubbish!" said Alice. "You're nothing but a pack of cards!" Then, to Alice's surprise, she woke up to find herself back on the riverbank. It had just been a dream after all!

Titles in this series include: